Aesop & Company

WITH SCENES FROM HIS LEGENDARY LIFE

Prepared by Barbara Bader   Pictured by Arthur Geisert

HOUGHTON MIFFLIN COMPANY

BOSTON   1991

For Steve — A.G.

Library of Congress Cataloging-in-Publication Data

Bader, Barbara.
 Aesop & company : with scenes from his legendary life / prepared
by Barbara Bader ; pictured by Arthur Geisert.
     p.   cm.
 Summary: A collection of concise stories told by the Greek slave,
Aesop. Includes facts and legends about his life and commentary on
the timeless appeal of his fables.
 ISBN 0-395-50597-6
 1. Fables. [1. Fables.] I. Geisert, Arthur, ill.   II. Aesop's
fables.   III. Title.   IV. Title: Aesop and company.
PZ8.2.B14Ae   1990   90-4838
398.24'52—dc20   CIP
                         AC

Printed in the United States of America

HOR 10 9 8 7 6 5 4 3 2 1

Contents

Introduction

Who Aesop Was and How the Fables Became World Famous

SOUR GRAPES. In union is strength. The lion's share. Cry wolf.

In language after language these are famous words, everyday expressions loaded with meaning. They come to us in the name of Aesop, an ancient Greek who never published a book and may not have set down a word in writing. We cannot be certain which of the hundreds of fables attributed to him he actually told. Indeed, so little is definitely known about Aesop that many have questioned his very existence.

How did this phantom personage come to be the best-known, most-quoted author of all time? The only author, too, whose name is synonymous with an entire narrative genre. Say Aesop, think fables; say fables, think Aesop.

In sixth century B.C. Greece, while Sappho was composing sublime love lyrics and Solon giving Athens its laws, word also spread of Aesop the fable-maker, the

fabulist. Once a slave on the island of Samos off Asia Minor, he was given his freedom by his master, Iadmon. This much we have reliably from Herodotus and his fellow historian Eugeon, both of whom lived on Samos after Aesop's time. All else is disputed — Aesop's place of birth, his reported travels and service to kings, his place and manner of death.

If the facts of Aesop's life are scant, there is abundant evidence of his prominence as a maker and teller of fables. Aristophanes, Plato, Aristotle, Xenophon, and others ascribe fables to him or suggest that on a certain occasion he might have contrived a fable to fit. He is linked by Plato to Socrates. In prison awaiting death, writes Plato, Socrates put Aesop's fables into verse. He had them "at hand," memorized.

To Herodotus and others, Aesop was not only "the fabulist," he was one-of-a-kind, the only fabulist worth speaking of. Probably no one before him had employed fables so extensively to make a point, the Aesop specialist Ben Perry surmises. And no one else used them so continually or so skillfully, a Greek near-contemporary testifies. Thus fables from here, there, and everywhere attached to his name.

But not only was the fable not invented by Aesop, it did not originate in Greece. Moreover, a fable is neither a moral tale nor a form of popular entertainment. Those were later developments, not part of the fable's original purpose.

Until quite recently scholars were inclined to trace the Greek fables associated with Aesop to a dual source in Greek folklore and Indian literary fables, the so-called Fables of Bidpai. Such was the widely credited contention of British folklorist Joseph Jacobs. But publication of new Sumerian discoveries in the 1950s demolished that theory. Here, on cuneiform tablets from 1800 B.C. or earlier, were fables identical in form, and occasionally even in substance, to those of Aesop. Ancient Sumerians were educated city dwellers with laws and a concept of justice — predecessors of sixth century B.C. Greeks. The line of descent runs clear and plain through the ancient Near East to the fall of the Assyrian Empire at the end of the seventh century B.C., and thence through the Greek colonies of Asia Minor to mainland Greece. Greek folklore did indeed supply subject matter; of Indian influence there is no apparent sign, early or late.

The Sumerian fables, like the characteristic fables of Aesop, are brief stories intended to illustrate a truth — stories "made up for the purpose of conveying an idea indirectly . . . instead of explicitly." This is Perry's definition of a fable, and it cannot be bettered or gainsaid.

Aesop did not spin tale after tale to enthrall or amuse an audience; he was no fireside spellbinder, no cracker-barrel wit. In a particular situation, he told a fable to win an argument or decide an issue. Many of his fables, including some of the best known, are about animals and animals only; but many, including "The Boy Who Cried Wolf" and "The Bundle of Sticks" in this selection, are not. Nor do they preach; they do not advocate moral behavior or show the ethical thing to do. Rather, they offer counsels of prudence and practical wisdom — how to avoid being cheated ("The Lion's Share"); how double-dealing may backfire ("The Fox

and the Stork"); and how pride may lead to a fall ("The Frog and the Ox").

If the shoe fit, others could use the fable, too. Thus the orator and scholar Demetrius first recorded the fables in the fourth century B.C. as a handbook for writers and speakers.

In the handbook format, each fable was preceded by a brief interpretation of its meaning, separate and indented, to indicate how the fable could be used, and thereby save readers the trouble of reading the whole. "He who goes after what belongs to another deservedly loses his own" ushers in the fable of the dog and the piece of meat in one such collection. The introductory tip-off became the concluding moral as we know it when subsequent collectors, especially those who put the fables into verse, began to think of themselves as literary persons with a message.

In Demetrius's collection the fables were in prose. But to the ancient Greeks only poetry was literature. Poetry was for reading, furthermore, not simply for reference; and its moral message was for everyone, regardless of circumstance.

The first to actually put Aesop into verse, as far as we know, were the Romanized Greek Phaedrus (writing in Latin) and the Hellenized Roman Babrius (writing in Greek), two minor poets whose books appeared respectively in the mid and late first century B.C. As poets, they claimed literary standing for their works — a status fully achieved only in the seventeenth century by the French poet-fabulist Jean de La Fontaine.

The genealogy of fable texts through the Middle Ages and after is a scholarly thicket we need not enter here. Suffice it to say that Aesop was first translated into English by William Caxton, England's first printer, from a French translation of a massive, heterogeneous German compilation that was substantially based on Latin prose reworkings of Phaedrus's Latin verse.

Legends of Aesop's life had sprung up by the time of Herodotus in the next century, one reason the facts are so hard to sort out. The legends proliferated until, around the first century B.C., they were strung together into an anonymous fictive biography entitled *Life of Aesop.* In it, Aesop appears the most contemptible of human creatures, a dwarfish monstrosity who cannot speak; but he proves himself to be a sharp, ingenious fellow. He wins the power of speech from a priestess of the goddess Isis. He repeatedly outwits his master, a professional philosopher; by interpreting a sign that has his master stumped, he gains his freedom. None less than Croesus, the great Persian king, determines to have his counsel. Other kings enlist his aid as well. Finally, Aesop is framed by the Delphians, jealous keepers of the oracle, and put to death.

The legendary *Life of Aesop* stands in classicist Perry's words as "one of the few genuinely popular books that have come down to us from ancient times." It accompanied the fables throughout the Middle Ages and beyond, and appears in Caxton's collection. An 1865 American edition of Aesop proclaims that "His life . . . is here faithfully presented to the public."

The Aesop it portrays is the Aesop of folklore: the lowliest of humans who triumphs by native wit over philosophers and kings. The voice of the people, leveled against the tyranny and arrogance of their superiors.

Still, the fables were never the special property of peasants and rebels, or of any one class or faction. Kings passed them on to their sons for instruction in wise rule. They were enlisted on both sides in the English struggle between king and Parliament, "Papists" and Protestants. Martin Luther retranslated them — along with his work on the psalms and the prophets — to replace the prevailing, morally lax German version. In czarist and Stalinist Russia, the fables of Aesop and others served as subversive weapons against a repressive regime: Russia had its own La Fontaine in Krylov, and it has a tradition of satirical fables to this day. But familiar Aesopic fables have also been called tools of American capitalism —

teaching nineteenth-century American schoolchildren to emulate the persistence of the tortoise and the diligence of the ant.

Young princes, young pupils. Apparently even a child could understand Aesop. Writing in the first century A.D., Quintilian, the Roman orator and teacher of rhetoric, recommended the use of fables with even the youngest pupils. "Let them learn first to tell the fables orally in clear, unpretentious language, then to write them out with the same simplicity of style; first putting the verses into prose and translating the substance in different words, then paraphrasing it more freely . . . so long as they preserve the poet's meaning."

Quintilian's inspired pedagogy, rediscovered during the Renaissance, was echoed by the Dutch humanist Erasmus, albeit with a distinctly didactic purpose. In *The Education of a Christian Prince,* Erasmus writes: "When the little fellow has listened with pleasure to Aesop's fable of the lion and the mouse . . . and when he has finished his laugh, then the teacher should point out the *new* moral: the . . . fable teaches the prince to despise no one . . . for no one is so weak that on occasion he may be a help to you."

Erasmus's enthusiasm for Aesop influenced educational practices in England and also had a hand in the reforms urged by the political philosopher John Locke, author of *An Essay Concerning Human Understanding,* and practicing pedagogue, in the late seventeenth century. Nothing was better than Aesop for children to begin with, said Locke — nothing more certain to hold their interest, more "apt to delight and entertain a Child . . . yet afford useful Reflection to a grown Man."

Thanks in part to champions like these, the fables became the common coin of European childhood. At school, the fables helped teach beginners their Greek and Latin and, in their native tongue, how to speak and write effectively. In the classroom and by the family hearth, they taught either good behavior or wise behavior, depending on the interpreter. Fittingly, most of them were about animals. Locke in particular made much of this advantage. They were serious and they were fun.

They were also suitable for illustration, another point in their favor to Locke. "If {a child's} Aesop has pictures in it, it will entertain him the better, and encourage him to read" by allowing him to identify words with objects, "Ideas being not . . . had from Sounds; but from the things themselves or their Pictures."

Locke's thinking accorded with the new educational psychology of the Czech theologian and pedagogue Comenius, whose *Orbis Pictus* launched picture books and pictorial instruction for children. But the visual possibilities of Aesop were perceived long before the advent of the printed book, and without regard to children.

The most tantalizing example is the very first. Pictured on an Athenian vase dating to the fifth century B.C., the time of Herodotus and Socrates, are a fox and a bunch of grapes. The fox is stalking off in high dudgeon and the grapes dangle beyond his reach. Aesop could be illustrated with a single, unmistakable image.

Similar shorthand illustrations of Aesop appear in medieval manuscripts and decorate the borders of the Bayeux Tapestry. But it was the printed book that brought the fables into mansion and cottage, academy and parish school. And these proliferating editions came with pictures. No other text, notes the art historian John McKendry, "has been illustrated so often, so diversely, and so continuously."

The fables are good to illustrate for many of the same reasons they are good to tell and to hear, and easy to remember. Everything is simplified. Often there are only two characters; if more, they fall into groups. The action is concentrated, usually focused on one crucial act. Detail is graphic, concrete, integral.

Yet the very conciseness of the texts affords scope for the illustrator. The fables are bound to no particular time or place; artists can choose any setting that suits them, or none at all. Detail can be sparse or plentiful. And, much more than the adaptor, the illustrator can stamp the tale with a distinctive style, a fresh perspective.

Young Americans took the fables as they found them, with crude woodcuts or lavishly embellished, and they found them everywhere.

Aesop was a colonial best seller in the edition attuned to the Puritan cause in

England. He was on the curriculum of America's first college preparatory school, Boston Latin. He was the backbone of the Spellers, which took children through their letters and on to simple reading exercises. He became a staple of nineteenth-century Readers, in which his morals were emphasized. He circulated widely on the frontier. A backwoods household might have had only a handful of books, but along with Bunyan's *Pilgrim's Progress* and the Bible would often be *Aesop's Fables.*

Lincoln knew the fables by heart. Dennis Hanks, Lincoln's half-brother, recalled young Abe reading them aloud of an evening. The barnyard anecdotes he later told in courtrooms, on the stump, and in the White House alike — more than a hundred are recorded — became instructive fables in the telling. Lincoln's hallmark as a storyteller, remarks the folklorist Richard Dorson, was "his application of the yarn to an immediate social or political situation."

Sometimes Lincoln referred to Aesop directly. Appealing for party unity in the 1853 election, he first cited Aesop's fable of the bundle of sticks, then invoked the Biblical phrase he would soon make famous in another context, "a house divided against itself cannot stand." Urged to give up Fort Sumter, he reminded his listener of Aesop's fable of the lion and the woodman's daughter: To win permission to marry her, the lion gives up his long teeth and his claws; and now

unarmed, he gets a beating instead of a bride. "May it not be so with me," said Lincoln, "if I give up all that is asked?"

Aesop also entered the American bloodstream, and flowed through it, by less conventional means. In print and by word of mouth, he made his way around the world, often turning into folklore in the process.

In sixteenth-century Mexico, long before Jamestown or Plymouth was founded, Aesop's fables were translated from Spanish into Nahuatl, the Aztec language, under missionary auspices, and from there they migrated north. (In Nahuatl, the fox became a coyote, the cock an indigenous turkey.) From other sources, written and oral, they turn up as local hunting yarns in Michigan's Northern Peninsula and among tales told by the Ojibway of northern Minnesota — where the turtle and rabbit race on ice, and the turtle plops into a hole and swims underneath, coming up through holes along the way to check on the rabbit's progress.

The fables reached Japan by way of Spanish and Portuese missionaries only slightly after their appearance in Mexico, and thrived. *Esopono Fabulas* was the only important nonreligious work translated into Japanese in the brief period before Christianity was suppressed and priests were expelled. Selections were reprinted time and again for the next 250 years, despite the virtual ban on Western writing.

In black Africa the fables survive as plot patterns, assimilated into native animal tales pitting the smart against the stupid, the wily against the ingenuous. (Aesop's fame rubbed off nonetheless on Joel Chandler Harris's black Georgian, Uncle Remus.) In the Philippines they reappear, practically intact, in native guise: The fox and the crow are a squirrel and a hawk, and the piece of cheese both covet is a salted fish.

Truly, as G. K. Chesterton said, Aesop is universal. He is more pervasive, perhaps, for the absence of hard fact that would make him a historical figure and limit the fables to a few specimens of ancient Greek thought. Unknown, he is unbounded.

Carnes, Pack. *Fable Scholarship: An Annotated Bibliography.* New York: Garland Publishing, 1985.

Daly, Lloyd William. *Aesop Without Morals.* New York: Thomas Yoseloff, 1961.

McKendry, John. *Aesop: Five Centuries of Illustrated Fables*. New York: Metropolitan Museum of Art, 1964.

Perry, Ben Edwin. *Babrius and Phaedrus*. Cambridge: Harvard University Press, 1965.

Perry, Ben Edwin. "Fable." *Studium Generale* 2 (1959): 17–37.

Provenzo, Eugene Francis, Jr. "Education and the Aesopic Tradition." Unpublished dissertation, Washington University, St. Louis, 1976.

The fables are adapted from Perry's prose translations of Babrius and Phaedrus and from recent translations, by Daly and others, of early prose collections traceable to Demetrius.

Arthur Geisert's illustrations are set in and around Galena, Illinois, where he lives.

Aesop & Company

The Tortoise and the Hare

———————

A HARE, BOASTING of his speed, was boldly challenged by a tortoise to a race. How ridiculous, thought the hare. But he agreed on a time and a place.

Confident of his greater speed, the hare was in no hurry. He ran a short way, then lay down beside the road and went to sleep.

The tortoise never slackened his pace. He passed the sleeping hare and plodded along, slow but sure, until he crossed the finish line and won the race.

Steady effort gains more than talent that isn't used.

The Dog with a Piece of Meat

A DOG WAS on his way home with a piece of meat, carrying it in his jaws the way dogs do, when he came to a bridge over a stream.

He started across, then stopped to look down over the edge. In the water below he saw another dog, with another, seemingly larger, piece of meat.

"I must have that piece of meat," thought the dog to himself.

So, without thinking twice, he opened his jaws to snatch the second piece of meat — and found himself with no meat at all. His own piece fell into the stream and disappeared. And the second piece, of course, was merely a reflection of the first.

In our greed for more we may lose what we already have.

The Fox and the Grapes

BACK IN THE days when foxes ate grapes, a hungry fox spied a bunch of grapes hanging from a lofty branch.

He took a leap, then another and another. It was no use. He couldn't reach the grapes.

"Never mind," said the fox to himself, turning away. "Those grapes are probably sour, anyhow."

It's easy to scorn what you can't get.

The North Wind and the Sun

THE NORTH WIND and the Sun were arguing over which of them was stronger when a peasant approached, clutching a goatskin cloak around his shoulders.

Here was a way to settle the argument. The test of strength, they decided, would be to strip the cloak from the fellow's back.

The North Wind went first. He blew hard, trying to remove the cloak by sheer force. But the peasant, shivering, only pulled the cloak closer.

It was the Sun's turn to try. First he shone gently, bringing the peasant welcome relief from the cold, raw wind. He relaxed his grip on the goatskin. Then little by little, the Sun increased his heat, until the peasant gladly threw off the cloak of his own accord.

Persuasion may accomplish more than force.

The Shepherd Boy who Cried "Wolf"

A SHEPHERD BOY, alone all day, got bored tending his sheep. To stir up a little excitement — and because he liked playing jokes — he shouted, "Wolf! Wolf!"

The villagers came running in alarm, only to find the shepherd boy laughing at them.

Again, some days later, the shepherd boy raised the cry of "Wolf! Wolf!" And again the villagers were deceived.

In time, as luck would have it, some wolves really did come. The shepherd boy called "Wolf! Wolf!" as loudly as he could, but no one paid the least attention. The villagers were not about to be fooled again.

Nobody believes a liar even when he tells the truth.

Belling the Cat

THE MICE ONCE held a meeting to discuss how to outwit their enemy, the cat.

Some suggested this, some suggested that. At last a wise old mouse stood up to speak. "You all know," said he, "that the danger lies in the sly way the cat approaches, without making a sound. If we could hear her coming, we could easily escape." Yes, that was so, the others agreed.

"Therefore," the old mouse continued, "let us get a small bell and hang it by a ribbon around the neck of the cat. Then we shall always know when she is on the prowl."

The mice nodded approvingly. "Very clever," said a young mouse. "But tell me this: Which one of us is going to tie on the ribbon? Just who will bell the cat?"

The mice looked at one another. "Not I, certainly," said one. "Nor I," said another. And a third piped up, "I wouldn't go near that cat for the world."

Easier said than done.

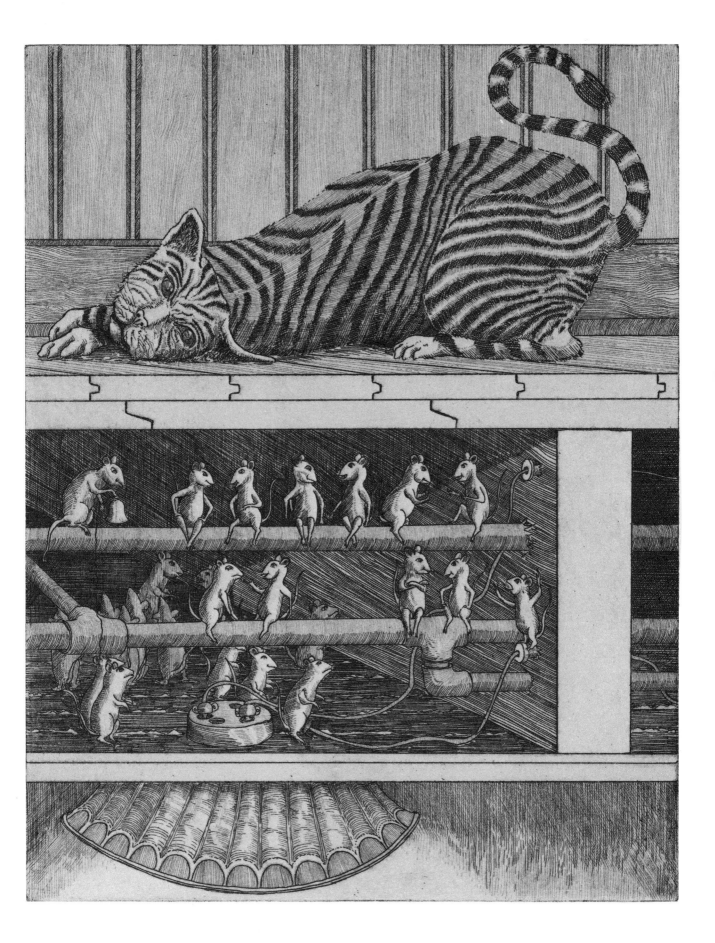

The Ant and the Grasshopper

A GRASSHOPPER WAS singing away one summer's day when an ant came plodding by, bent under the weight of a kernel of corn.

"Why work so hard in this fine warm weather?" the grasshopper called to the ant. "Why not enjoy yourself, like me?"

"I'm storing up food for the winter," the ant replied. "And I suggest you do the same."

"Winter!" scoffed the grasshopper. "Who cares about winter! We have more food than we can eat."

The ant held his tongue and went about his business.

Then winter set in, and soon the grasshopper couldn't find so much as a grain of barley or wheat. He went to the ant to beg for some food, knowing the ant had plenty.

"Friend grasshopper," said the ant, "you sang while I slaved away last summer, and laughed at me besides. Sing now and see what it will get you."

Save for the future and you won't be without.

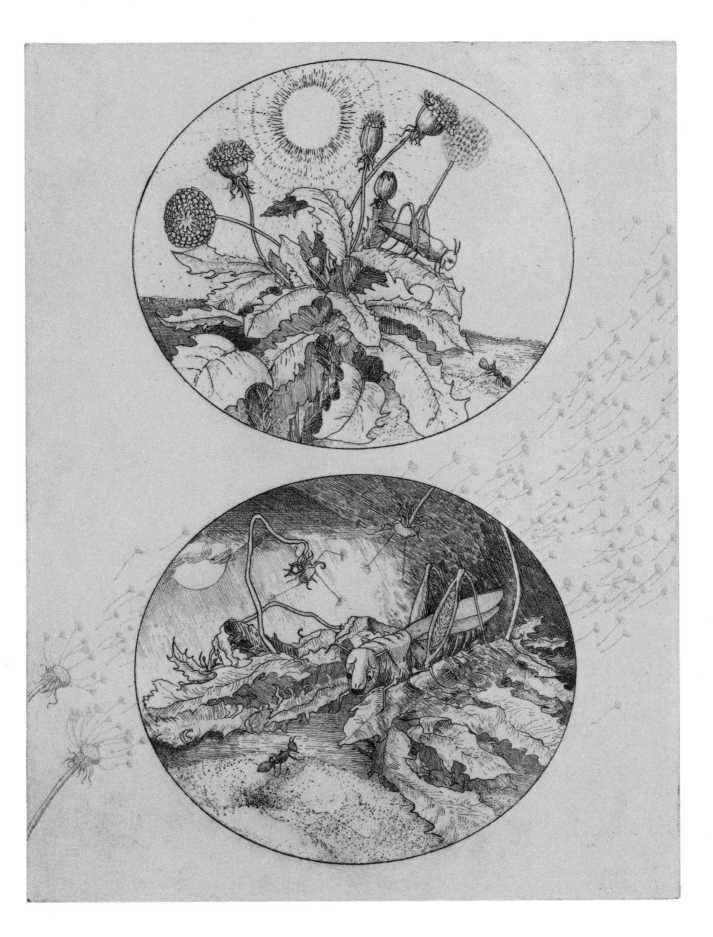

The Lion and the Mouse

A MOUSE RAN over the body of a sleeping lion. The lion awoke, seized the mouse, and was about to eat him.

"Oh, sir," cried the mouse, "a stag or a bull is a fit meal for you, not a puny mouse. If you spare me I may be able to return the favor someday, small as I am."

The lion smiled and let the mouse go.

One day the lion was caught in a hunter's net. Hearing his groans, the mouse rushed to his side. With his tiny teeth he gnawed at the net until he set the lion free.

Little friends may prove to be great friends.

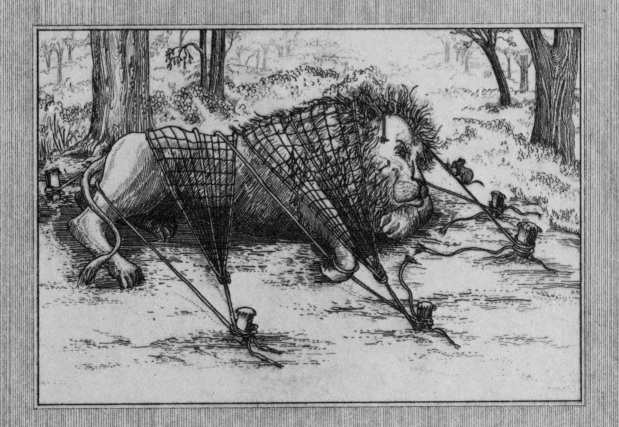

The Fox and the Cat

A FOX WAS boasting to a cat about the many clever ways he had of escaping from his enemies. "When dogs chase me," he said, "I have a whole bag of tricks to give them the slip. And what about you?"

The cat had to admit that she had only one way to assure her safety. "When dogs pursue me," she said, "I scramble up into a tree."

Just then the two heard a pack of dogs approaching. The cat trembled, and the fox could not decide which trick to use.

"I can't wait," said the cat. And up into a tree she went.

Seeing the cat escape, the dogs set upon the hesitating fox and quickly caught him, while the cat sat safely on her high perch.

You can always count on the tried-and-true.

The Crow and the Pitcher

A THIRSTY CROW came upon a pitcher half-filled with water. But the water was too low for him to reach.

He pushed and pushed, trying to tip the pitcher over, but still the pitcher stood.

The crow stopped to think, and caught sight of some pebbles. One by one he picked them up and dropped them into the pitcher. Slowly, slowly, the level of the water rose . . . until the crow was able to put his beak in and drink his fill.

Use your head, not just your muscle.

The Frogs who Wanted a King

SOME FROGS ONCE grew troubled at having no one to rule over them and keep them in line. So they asked the mighty god Zeus to provide them with a king.

Laughing at their stupidity, Zeus dropped a log into their pond, where it landed with a great *splash!* That was the right king for them.

The frogs, taking fright, dove to the bottom of the pond. Then one frog stuck his head up. When he saw that the log lay quite still, he called the other frogs. Soon they were all perched on the log, perfectly at ease.

As a ruler, however, this blockhead did not please the frogs. So they asked Zeus for another king, a properly strict one who would lay down the law. And this time Zeus sent them a water snake, who devoured every one of them he could catch.

Beware of trading freedom for tyranny.

The Wolf and the Lamb

A THIRSTY WOLF and a thirsty lamb came to the same stream to drink. Upstream stood the wolf; farther down stood the lamb. But the wolf, who had a taste for tender young meat, was not about to let the lamb be.

"Why," said he, "have you muddied the water where I'm drinking?"

"How could I?" answered the lamb. "The water flows downstream from you to me."

"Hmpf," said the wolf, quiet for a moment. "But why did you curse me, six months back?"

"How could I?" answered the lamb. "Six months ago I wasn't even born."

"Well," the wolf went on, "if it wasn't you, it must have been your father."

And with that he pounced upon the lamb and ate him up.

For a scoundrel, any excuse will do.

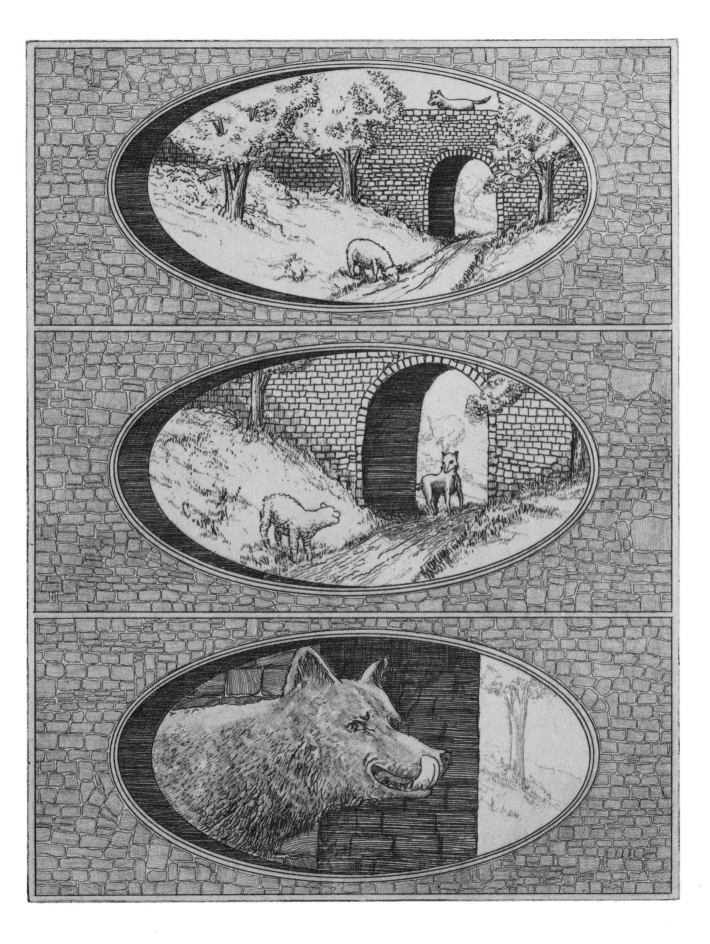

The Fox and the Stork

A FOX INVITED a stork to dinner, and set before her some thin soup in a flat saucer. With her long thin bill, the stork could not get so much as a taste, while the fox lapped up the soup with relish.

In return, the stork invited the fox to dinner. When he arrived, she served him a narrow-mouthed jar full of solid food. Hungry as he was, the fox could only watch as the stork thrust her bill into the jar and ate until she could eat no more.

Tit for tat.

The Bundle of Sticks

AN ELDERLY FARMER, nearing death, was troubled by the quarreling of his sons. He reasoned with them; he reproached them. But still they quarreled. So he decided to translate words into action.

He called them to his bedside, and told them to fetch a bundle of sticks.

"Boys," he said, "take this bundle and try to break the sticks in two."

One tried, and then another. But no matter how hard they tried, the bundle held firm. They could not break the sticks.

The farmer undid the bundle and separated the sticks. He gave one stick to each son. "Now," he said, "try again."

The sticks broke easily.

"It's the same with you, boys," said their father. "If you stay together, no one will be able to do you any harm — but if you quarrel, your enemies will destroy you."

In union is strength.

The Young Crab and
Her Mother

———————

ONE DAY A mother crab took her young daughter for a walk on the beach, wiggling across the sand in the curious way that crabs have.

The young crab did likewise.

"Child," said the mother crab, "you are not walking properly. You must learn to walk straight forward without twisting from side to side."

"If you walk straight yourself, mother," the young crab replied, "I will try to do the same."

A good example is the best teacher.

The Country Mouse and the City Mouse

A COUNTRY MOUSE and a city mouse decided to share their different ways of life with one another.

First the city mouse came to visit his country friend. Corn and barley and fresh milk were the only food for dinner, but the country mouse served them up freely in his snug home.

The city mouse looked down his nose at such modest arrangements. "It's the life of an ant you live, my friend," said he, "eating off the land and living underground. By comparison, I live like a prince. You shall see for yourself."

Off they started, arriving in the city at dusk. The city mouse led the way under a wall and up into a glittering room. The remains of a lavish meal stood on the sideboard. The country mouse was envious, and admitted it. But they had hardly begun to eat when somebody suddenly threw open a door, sending the frightened mice scampering for the nearest hole.

That was enough for the country mouse. "Goodbye, my friend," he said. "You may have your fine feasts to yourself. I'll stick to my simple fare and enjoy it in peace."

Better a morsel in peace than a banquet in fear.

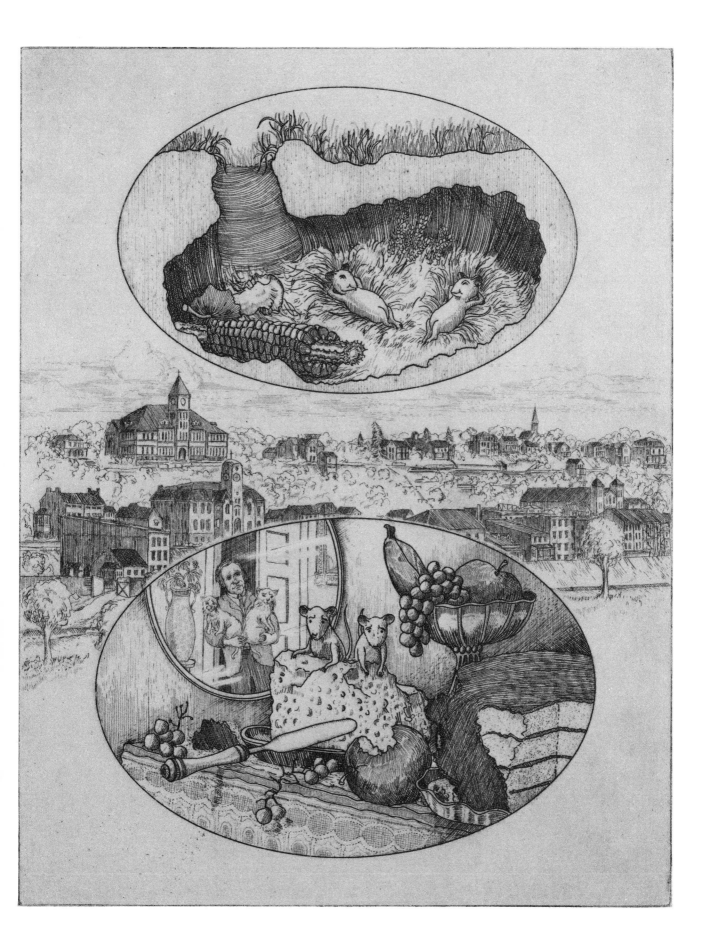

The Frog and the Ox

AN OX, DRINKING at a stream, accidentally stepped on a baby frog. The mother frog was away at the time. On her return she asked his brothers and sisters what had happened to him.

"Oh, mother," they said, shuddering. "While you were gone a huge four-footed beast came by and trampled on him."

The mother frog puffed herself up and asked, "A beast as big as this?"

"Bigger," they said.

Puffing harder, she inflated herself still more. "As big as this?" she asked again.

"Stop, mother," the children cried. "You'll burst before you get to be as big as that beast."

But, alas, the mother did not listen. She puffed and puffed, and blew herself up until finally she exploded.

Never try to be more than you are.

The Fox and the Crow

A CROW STOOD perched on a high branch, holding a piece of cheese in his beak. A crafty fox came by and hankered for that piece of cheese for himself.

"Sir Crow," called the fox, "you have beautiful wings and bright, keen eyes. You have the breast of an eagle and matchless claws. If only you had a voice, you might be king of the birds."

Eager to prove that he did indeed have a voice, the foolish crow let go of the cheese and croaked, "Caw! Caw!"

The fox snatched up the fallen cheese. "You do indeed have a voice," he called. "You seem to have everything, Sir Crow, except a brain."

Don't let flattery go to your head.

The Lion's Share

A FOX AND an ass became partners with a lion, and the three went out together to hunt.

They made a big killing, and the lion divided the meat into three equal shares.

"This first portion," he said, "I shall take for myself because I am the king of beasts. And I shall take this second portion also, because I am partners with you on equal terms."

The lion paused briefly.

"As for the third portion," he concluded, "I should like to see which one of you would dare to claim it."

Leave it to a lion to take the lion's share.

Life of Aesop

Early Episodes from the Legendary Life of Aesop

Tales about Aesop's remarkable life were passed down for centuries, along with his fables. Because people had almost no facts to go on, they accepted these legends as truth. It was easy to think of Aesop, the ancient Greek who made up such clever fables, as an extraordinary fellow.

How Aesop Won the Power of Speech

Aesop the great fabulist was once a slave of the philosopher Xanthus, on the island of Samos. Even among slaves he was a figure of scorn. Nature had given Aesop a large, misshapen head on a dwarfish body, a hump back, bow legs, and a potbelly. Worst of all, Aesop was unable to speak.

His fellow slaves took advantage of his affliction to blame their own misdeeds on him. After all, they reasoned, Aesop could not defend himself. But Aesop was cleverer than they. Falsely accused of eating his master's figs, Aesop drank a basin of water, put his fingers down his throat, and threw up clear water. Then he insisted that his accusers do the same. Out came the figs, proving Aesop's innocence.

The following day, as he was working in the fields, Aesop was approached by a priestess of the mother god Isis, who had lost her way. "Good fellow," she said, "I beg of you to show me the road to the city, for I am a stranger and lost."

Seeing by his gestures that he could hear but could not speak, the priestess let Aesop lead her to a nearby grove of tress. He shared his lunch of bread and olives with her, then led her to a spring of water for a drink. When she was ready to go, Aesop showed her the road to the city.

On her way again, the priestess raised her arms to Isis and asked that Aesop be rewarded. Let him be given the power of speech, she prayed. Isis listened, for the ears of the gods are always open to words of kindness to others and reverence for themselves.

Meanwhile, Aesop lay down in the grass to rest. He drifted off to sleep to the whispering of a stream and the songs of many birds.

As he slept Isis appeared with the nine Muses, who preside over the arts and sciences. "My daughters," she said, "here is a man ill-favored by nature but beyond reproach for his behavior. I will restore his voice. You will endow him with the mastery of language and invention."

With that, the goddess removed the impediment from Aesop's tongue, and the Muses conferred upon him the talents of a storyteller. Isis ordained that he achieve fame, and then departed, and soon the Muses too were gone.

When Aesop awoke he began, without thinking, to name the things that he saw: napkin, pouch, ox, ass, sheep. And he realized he had the power of speech. But where had it come from? Surely from the gods. And Aesop rejoiced.

He was not long in putting his new power to use. Coming upon the overseer beating a slave, Aesop berated him. "Why do you mistreat a man who has done no wrong?" asked Aesop. "You often do wrong and are not beaten for it." The astonished overseer rushed to his master's house to report that Aesop, that ugly wretch, could now speak, and was saying terrible things. He would be a plague to them all.

Aesop and his Master Match Wits

And indeed, Aesop's master, Xanthus, was soon tearing his hair at the things Aesop said. Aesop was proving himself cleverer than Xanthus, a philosopher by training and trade.

One day the two went to a local garden to buy vegetables, and the gardener asked Xanthus about something that had been troubling him: "Why is it that when I put plants in the ground and then hoe them and water them and give

them all kinds of attention, the weeds still come up before the things I've planted?"

Xanthus, stumped for an immediate answer, spoke vaguely of the divine order of nature, which was beyond study or reasoning. At that, Aesop laughed.

"Suppose you try to answer the question," said Xanthus.

"Well," said Aesop, "it's like a woman with both children of her own and stepchildren. She loves her own more, and bestows the best of everything on them. The earth is the same. She is a mother to the plants that grow spontaneously but a stepmother to the ones you plant. So she favors her own, and they flourish."

The gardener, well satisfied, insisted that they accept his vegetables as a gift.

Aesop's Lesson in Giving Orders

In time, Xanthus decided to be strict with Aesop. He ordered him to do only what he was told, no more and no less. "Get the oil flask and the towels," Xanthus said, "and let's go to the bath."

Aesop decided to teach Xanthus a lesson. When Xanthus asked for the oil flask, that is exactly what he got — an empty flask. When Xanthus told Aesop

to hurry home and "cook lentil" for his friends, Aesop did. He served a single lentil in a pot of water.

To make amends to his friends, Xanthus told Aesop to cook the four pig's feet he had bought. Secretly he planned to trick Aesop and put him in the wrong, so he could give him a thrashing. When Aesop had put the pig's feet in a kettle to cook, Xanthus sent him on an errand. He then removed one of the pig's feet and hid it. On his return Aesop saw through the trick. He went into the yard, cut a foot off the pig that was being saved for dinner on Xanthus's wife's birthday, and threw it into the kettle. But Xanthus, worried that Aesop might run away if he found a foot missing, sneaked the stolen foot back into the kettle. That made five pig's feet. But Aesop didn't know there were five feet in the kettle, and neither did Xanthus.

When it came time to serve the pig's feet, out of the kettle came five feet. Xanthus turned pale and said, "Aesop, how many feet did that pig have?"

"It works out all right, master," Aesop replied. "Here are five feet, and the pig outside has three."

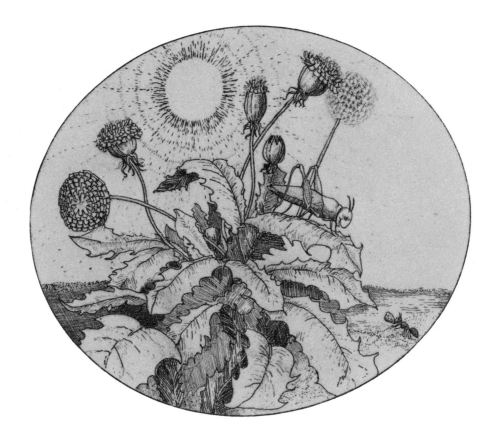

Xanthus was beside himself with rage.

It was his own fault, Aesop told him, for laying down the law so literally. And the next time Xanthus gave orders, he was careful to add to his instructions, "And anything else I may have forgotten."

How Aesop Gained his Freedom

Aesop could be infuriating, but he was also extremely useful. So Xanthus would not hear of giving him his freedom.

"Just you wait and see, master," Aesop said. "Whether you like it or not, one day you will set me free."

About this time the citizens of Samos assembled for a meeting. Suddenly an eagle swooped down, seized the city seal from the book of laws, and flew away. An evil portent, the Samians decided. But what did it mean?

Xanthus was called upon. He asked for time to ponder the meaning. As the people were about to leave, the eagle flew down again and deposited the seal in the lap of a public slave. Here was something else that called for an explanation.

Worried, Xanthus went home and summoned Aesop. But Aesop, who had recently been punished, was angry and pretended not to have an answer. Xanthus lost hope. Rather than face the Samians without an explanation and be shamed, he would hang himself. When Aesop saw him go out with a rope and attach it to a tree, he shouted, "Wait, master!"

He would interpret the portent, he told Xanthus. But they must call another public meeting, and Xanthus must introduce Aesop as his pupil.

At the sight of Aesop the Samians burst out laughing. Aesop, however, remained calm. He reminded them not to judge a man by his looks any more than they would judge a jar of wine before tasting it. Impressed by his cleverness and his gift for speaking, the Samians clamored for Aesop to interpret the eagle's theft and return of the city seal.

Now that he had won their favor, Aesop had something more to say. "A free

people should not have a slave interpret a portent. If I interpret it correctly, I should receive the honor due a free man; and if I am wrong, I should receive the punishment due a free man, as well."

The people begged Xanthus to free Aesop. When he refused, the leader of the meeting called out, "Accept the price you paid for him, and I'll make him a free man on behalf of the city."

Xanthus had paid very little for Aesop, and he did not want his stinginess made public. He brought Aesop forward and said, "Xanthus, at the request of the people of Samos, lets Aesop go free."

It happened just as Aesop had foretold. Now he was ready to interpret the portents. "Men of Samos, take counsel," he said. "The eagle who flew down is the king of the birds. He removed the seal, the symbol of leadership, from the book of laws and dropped it in the lap of a public slave. The meaning is plain: One of the ruling kings is determined to destroy your freedom, to abrogate your laws, and set the seal of his power upon you."

Even as Aesop spoke, an emissary arrived from Croesus, king of the Lydians, demanding tribute in return for protection. The Samians turned to Aesop; should they pay tribute or not? Instead of answering directly, Aesop replied with a fable: "On the one hand is the rough road of freedom, full of peril, which finally comes out on a fertile plain. On the other is the smooth path of servitude, which ends in a narrow crevice with no way out."

The Samians understood. They shouted to the emissary that they would take the rough road.

When Croesus heard the answer, he prepared to call up his army. But he was advised not to be hasty, for he would never conquer the Samians as long as Aesop was among them. Instead, he should demand the surrender of Aesop, and he did. Of his own accord, and for his own reasons, Aesop went.

He made himself invaluable to Croesus and to other rulers as well. The fame of his fables spread and endured, and his wisdom brought him renown as a benefactor of humankind.